A Trip with Grandma

Ruth Ohi

annick press
toronto + new york + vancouver

We acknowledge the support of the Canada Council for the Arts, the
Ontario Arts Council, and the Government of Canada through the Book
Publishing Industry Development Program (BPIDP) for our publishing
activities.

Cataloging in Publication

Ohi, Ruth
      A trip with Grandma / written and illustrated by Ruth Ohi.

"A Ruth Ohi picture book".
ISBN-13: 978-1-55451-072-6 (bound)
ISBN-13: 978-1-55451-071-9 (pbk.)
ISBN-10: 1-55451-072-4 (bound)
ISBN-10: 1-55451-071-6 (pbk.)

     1. Picture books for children. I. Title.

PS8579.H47T75 2007   jC813'.54   C2006-904413-9

The art in this book was rendered in watercolor.
The text was typeset in Cheltenham.

Distributed in Canada by: Published in the U.S.A. by:
Firefly Books Ltd.   Annick Press (U.S.) Ltd.
66 Leek Crescent   Distributed in the U.S.A. by:
Richmond Hill, ON   Firefly Books (U.S.) Inc.
L4B 1H1   P.O. Box 1338
                          Ellicott Station
                          Buffalo, NY 14205

Printed in China.

Visit us at: www.annickpress.com

For Annie and Sara's dearest Vanaema.
—R.O.

CLIK
CLIK

In all the
world there was
only one Sprout
quite like Sprout.

This is Flatmouse. He wants to be a construction worker train conductor airplane pilot when he grows up.

Sprout liked big trucks.

He liked long trains.

Sprout liked seeing new places, but he had never been away without Mom and Dad before – not even for a sleepover.

One day the telephone rang. It was Grandma. She wanted to take Sprout and his big sister, Clara, on a trip to Bumper's Valley.

That's where the tallest trees in the world are!

It was a fair drive away, so the three of them would stay overnight in a hotel.

Sprout was nervous.

He loved his Grandma, but he was more used to Mom and Dad.

The big day arrived. Grandma pulled her car into the driveway. Sprout stuck close to Clara and Flatmouse.

"We'll make sure we phone home a lot," said Grandma. "Mom and Dad might miss you otherwise."

Clara, Sprout, and Grandma drove past fields and farms and cows. Flatmouse buried his nose in Sprout's shirt.

"Shall we phone home," said Grandma
when they stopped for gas, "to tell them that
we found double chocolate ice cream?"
    Sprout nodded and reached for the phone.

Clara, Sprout, and Grandma drove past a silver lake and a black forest. Sprout held Flatmouse up to the window so that Flatmouse could see too.

"Shall we phone home," said Grandma when they stopped for a snack, "to tell them what we saw in the forest?"

Sprout nodded and reached for the phone.

Clara, Sprout, and Grandma drove
past 21 red cars, a giant moving tunnel,
and a truck with three dogs sticking out
of it, their ears waving.

And then they phoned home to tell Mom and Dad
that they had reached their hotel in Bumper's Valley.
"We're going to get dinner," said Clara to her parents.
"Someplace with dessert," added Sprout.

Dinner was at a place with dancing chickens. Sprout scowled when he saw the waiter bring a booster seat.

"Oh no, thank you," said Grandma to the waiter. "We won't be needing that."

Sprout beamed. "It can be for Flatmouse," he said.

Once back at the hotel, it was time for bed. Sprout was nervous. Clara, Sprout, and Grandma brushed their teeth and read a story about a frog who wished to be kissed by a princess.

"Can we phone home," asked Sprout, "to tell them we're going to sleep?"

Grandma thought that was a fine idea.

Sprout told Mom and Dad all about the dancing chickens. Mom and Dad laughed.

"Well," said Sprout, "good night."

"Good night," said Mom and Dad. "Love you."

"Love you, too," said Sprout.

"Now, please wake me up if I start snoring," said Grandma, tucking them in. "I don't want to keep you two from a good night's sleep."

Grandma and Clara fell asleep right away. Sprout couldn't. He heard strange sounds coming from Grandma's bed.

"Grandma," whispered Sprout. "You're snoring!"
Grandma rolled over. The snoring stopped.
"Thank you for telling me, Sprout," murmured
Grandma. "Good night."
"Good night," whispered Sprout.

A few minutes later, Sprout heard the sounds again. He went to Grandma's bed.

"Grandma?" whispered Sprout. "Are you snoring?"

"I must be," said Grandma, rolling over to face Sprout. "Thanks for waking me. Good night. Love you."

"Love you, too," said Sprout.

Sprout didn't go back to bed. He looked at Grandma.

"Grandma?" said Sprout. "Maybe I should sleep in your bed. That way I can tell you right away if you start snoring."

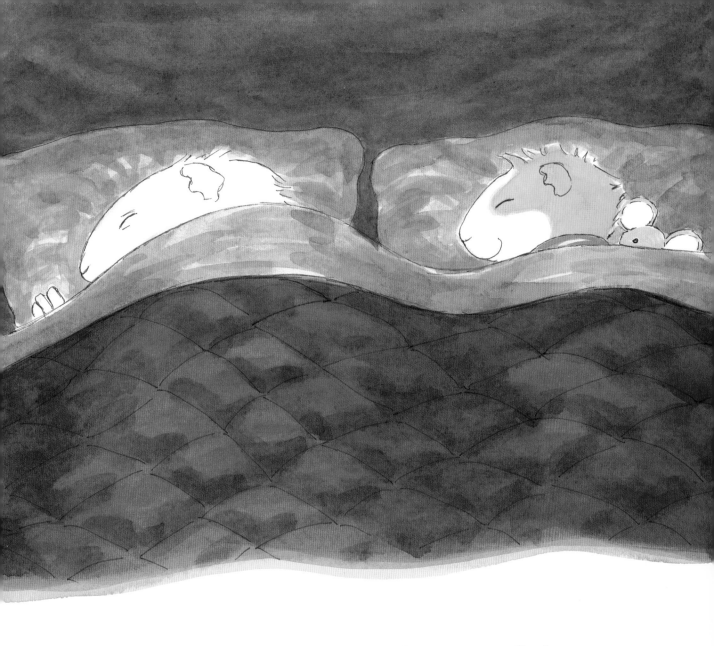

"Good idea," said Grandma, her eyes still shut.
Sprout crawled in next to her and soon fell asleep.

After breakfast the next day, it was time
to see the giant trees of Bumper's Valley.

"Shall we phone home," asked Grandma,
"and tell them we're off?"

"No," said Sprout, hugging Grandma.
"Let's just go!"

The trees were huge. Clara, Sprout, and Grandma felt very small.

"Trees are very quiet," said Sprout.
Grandma agreed.
They stayed until their stomachs grumbled.
"Time to eat," said Grandma.

After lunch, it was time to drive back home.
They stopped two times – once to get
peaches for Mom and again because Sprout
saw the perfect flying pig for Dad.

And then they were home.
Grandma gave Sprout and Clara a goodbye hug.
"Thanks for coming with me," said Grandma.
"I really enjoyed being with you."
"Me, too," said Sprout. "When can we go again?"